THIS BOOK

BELONGS TO:

....

....

THE TALE OF

The Pie and The
Patty-Pan

BUTTER AND MILK FROM THE FARM

THE TALE OF
THE PIE AND THE PATTY~PAN

BY

BEATRIX POTTER

A PETER RABBIT™

110th Anniversary Edition

FREDERICK WARNE

FREDERICK WARNE

Published by the Penguin Group
Penguin Books Ltd., 80 Strand, London WC2R 0RL, England
Penguin Group (USA) Inc., 375 Hudson Street, New York, New York 10014, USA
Penguin Group (Australia), 250 Camberwell Road, Camberwell,
Victoria 3124, Australia (a division of Pearson Australia Group Pty. Ltd.)
Penguin Group (Canada), 90 Eglinton Avenue East, Suite 700, Toronto,
Ontario M4P 2Y3, Canada (a division of Pearson Penguin Canada Inc.)
Penguin Books India Pvt. Ltd., 11 Community Centre, Panchsheel Park, New Delhi—110 017, India
Penguin Group (NZ), 67 Apollo Drive, Rosedale, Auckland 0632,
New Zealand (a division of Pearson New Zealand Ltd.)
Penguin Books (South Africa) (Pty.) Ltd, 24 Sturdee Avenue, Rosebank, Johannesburg 2196, South Africa

Penguin Books Ltd., Registered Offices: 80 Strand, London WC2R 0RL, England

Website: www.peterrabbit.com

First published by Frederick Warne in 1905
First published with reset text and new reproductions
of Beatrix Potter's illustrations in 2002
This edition published in 2011

003 - 10 9 8 7 6 5 4 3

New reproductions copyright © Frederick Warne & Co., 2002
Original copyright in text and illustrations © Frederick Warne & Co., 1905
Frederick Warne & Co. is the owner of all rights, copyrights and trademarks
in the Beatrix Potter character names and illustrations.

Colour reproduction by
EAE Creative Colour Ltd, Norwich
Printed and bound in China

PUBLISHER'S NOTE

The Pie and The Patty-Pan, as this story was originally titled, was Beatrix Potter's seventh book, and a departure from her previous work in terms of both content and presentation. Beatrix and her editor Norman Warne had already discussed the possibility of printing her books in a larger size (177 mm x 138 mm), and for *The Pie and The Patty-Pan* this format was adopted, in order to do justice to the colour and detail of the pictures.

Likewise, the text was revised from an original, simpler story in which Ribby and Duchess express polite shock at the news that someone has been stealing chickens and eggs from the local farm – and then eat chicken pie and eggs for their tea. Beatrix thought this too thin, and replaced it with the version we know today.

Pussy-cat sits by the fire —
How should she be fair?
In walks the little dog —
Says "Pussy are you there?
How do you do Mistress Pussy?
Mistress Pussy, how do you do?"
"I thank you kindly little dog,
I fare as well as you!"

OLD RHYME

Once upon a time there was a Pussy-cat called Ribby, who invited a little dog called Duchess, to tea.

"Come in good time, my dear Duchess," said Ribby's letter, "and we will have something so very very nice. I am baking it in a pie-dish — a pie-dish with a pink rim. You never tasted anything so good!

And *you* shall eat it all! *I* will eat muffins, my dear Duchess!" wrote Ribby.

Duchess read the letter and wrote an answer: "I will come with much pleasure at a quarter past four. But it is very strange. *I* was just going to invite you to come here, to supper, my dear Ribby, to eat something *most delicious*.

"I will come very punctually, my dear Ribby," wrote Duchess; and then at the end she added — "I hope it isn't mouse?"

And then she thought that did not look quite polite; so she scratched out "isn't mouse" and

THE INVITATION

changed it to "I hope it will be fine," and she gave her letter to the postman.

But she thought a great deal about Ribby's pie, and she read Ribby's letter over and over again.

"I am dreadfully afraid it *will* be mouse!" said Duchess to herself—"I really couldn't, *couldn't* eat mouse pie. And I shall have to eat it, because it is a party. And *my* pie was going to be veal and ham. A pink and white pie-dish! and so is mine; just like Ribby's dishes; they were both bought at Tabitha Twitchit's."

Duchess went into her larder

and took the pie off a shelf and
looked at it.

"It is all ready to put into the
oven. Such lovely pie-crust;
and I put in a little tin patty-
pan to hold up the crust; and

I made a hole in the middle with a fork to let out the steam — Oh I do wish I could eat my own pie, instead of a pie made of mouse!"

Duchess considered and considered and read Ribby's letter again —

"A pink and white pie-dish — and *you* shall eat it *all*. 'You' means me — then Ribby is not going to even taste the pie herself? A pink and white pie-dish! Ribby is sure to go out to buy the muffins ... Oh what a good idea! Why shouldn't I rush along and put my pie into Ribby's oven when Ribby isn't there?"

Duchess was quite delighted
with her own cleverness!

Ribby in the meantime had
received Duchess's answer, and as
soon as she was sure that the little
dog could come — she popped *her*
pie into the oven. There were two

ovens, one above the other; some other knobs and handles were only ornamental and not intended to open. Ribby put the pie into the lower oven; the door was very stiff.

"The top oven bakes too quickly," said Ribby to herself. "It is a pie of the most delicate and tender mouse minced up with bacon. And I have taken out all the bones; because Duchess did nearly choke herself with a fish-bone last time I gave a party. She eats a little fast — rather big mouthfuls. But a most genteel and elegant little dog; infinitely superior company to Cousin Tabitha Twitchit."

THE PIE MADE OF MOUSE

15

Ribby put on some coal and swept up the hearth. Then she went out with a can to the well, for water to fill up the kettle.

Then she began to set the room in order, for it was the sitting-room as well as the kitchen. She shook the mats out at the front door and put them straight; the hearth-rug was a rabbit-skin. She dusted the clock and the ornaments on the mantelpiece, and she polished and rubbed the tables and chairs.

Then she spread a very clean white tablecloth, and set out her best china tea-set, which she took out of a wall-cupboard near the fire-place. The tea-cups were white with a pattern of pink roses; and the dinner-plates were white and blue.

When Ribby had laid the table she took a jug and a blue and

white dish, and went out down the field to the farm, to fetch milk and butter.

When she came back, she peeped into the bottom oven; the pie looked very comfortable.

Ribby put on her shawl and bonnet and went out again with a basket, to the village shop to buy a packet of tea, a pound of lump sugar, and a pot of marmalade.

And just at the same time, Duchess came out of *her* house, at the other end of the village.

Ribby met Duchess half-way down the street, also carrying a basket, covered with a cloth.

THE VEAL AND HAM PIE

They only bowed to one another;
they did not speak, because they
were going to have a party.

As soon as Duchess had got
round the corner out of sight —
she simply ran! Straight away to
Ribby's house!

Ribby went into the shop and
bought what she required, and
came out, after a pleasant gossip
with Cousin Tabitha Twitchit.

Cousin Tabitha was disdainful
afterwards in conversation—

"A little *dog* indeed! Just as if
there were no CATS in Sawrey!

And a *pie* for afternoon tea! The very idea!" said Cousin Tabitha Twitchit.

Ribby went on to Timothy Baker's and bought the muffins. Then she went home.

There seemed to be a sort of scuffling noise in the back passage, as she was coming in at the front door.

"I trust that is not that Pie; the spoons are locked up, however," said Ribby.

But there was nobody there. Ribby opened the bottom oven door with some difficulty, and turned the pie. There began to be a

WHERE IS THE PIE MADE OF MOUSE?

pleasing smell of baked mouse!

Duchess in the meantime, had slipped out at the back door.

"It is a very odd thing that Ribby's pie was *not* in the oven when I put mine in! And I can't find it anywhere; I have looked all over the house. I put *my* pie into a nice hot oven at the top. I could not turn any of the other handles; I think that they are all shams," said Duchess, "but I wish I could have removed the pie made of mouse! I cannot think what she has done with it? I heard Ribby coming and I had to run out by the back door!"

Duchess went home and brushed her beautiful black coat; and then she picked a bunch of flowers in her garden as a present for Ribby; and passed the time until the clock struck four.

Ribby — having assured herself by careful search that there was really no one hiding in the cupboard or in the larder — went upstairs to change her dress.

She put on a lilac silk gown, for the party, and an embroidered muslin apron and tippet.

"It is very strange," said Ribby, "I did not *think* I left that drawer pulled out; has somebody been trying on my mittens?"

She came downstairs again, and made the tea, and put the teapot on the hob. She peeped again into the *bottom* oven; the pie had become a lovely brown, and it was steaming hot.

READY FOR THE PARTY

She sat down before the fire to wait for the little dog. "I am glad I used the *bottom* oven," said Ribby, "the top one would certainly have been very much too hot. I wonder why that cupboard door was open? Can there really have been someone in the house?"

Very punctually at four o'clock, Duchess started to go to the party. She ran so fast through the village that she was too early, and she had to wait a little while in the lane that leads down to Ribby's house.

"I wonder if Ribby has taken *my* pie out of the oven yet?" said Duchess, "and whatever can have

become of the other pie made of mouse?"

At a quarter past four to the minute, there came a most genteel little tap-tappity. "Is Mrs. Ribston at home?" inquired Duchess in the porch.

"Come in! and how do you do? my dear Duchess," cried Ribby. "I hope I see you well?"

"Quite well, I thank you, and how do *you* do, my dear Ribby?" said Duchess. "I've brought you some flowers; what a delicious smell of pie!"

"Oh, what lovely flowers! Yes, it is mouse and bacon!"

DUCHESS IN THE PORCH

"Do not talk about food, my dear Ribby," said Duchess; "what a lovely white tea-cloth! . . . Is it done to a turn? Is it still in the oven?"

"I think it wants another five minutes," said Ribby. "Just a shade longer; I will pour out the tea, while we wait. Do you take sugar, my dear Duchess?"

"Oh yes, please! my dear Ribby; and may I have a lump upon my nose?"

"With pleasure, my dear Duchess; how beautifully you beg! Oh, how sweetly pretty!"

Duchess sat up with the sugar on her nose and sniffed—

"How good that pie smells! I do
love veal and ham — I mean to say
mouse and bacon—"

She dropped the sugar in confusion, and had to go hunting under the tea-table, so she did not see which oven Ribby opened in order to get out the pie.

Ribby set the pie upon the table; there was a very savoury smell.

Duchess came out from under the tablecloth munching sugar, and sat up on a chair.

"I will first cut the pie for you; I am going to have muffin and marmalade," said Ribby.

"Do you really prefer muffin? Mind the patty-pan!"

"I beg your pardon?" said Ribby.

"May I pass you the marmalade?" said Duchess hurriedly.

The pie proved extremely tooth-some, and the muffins light and hot. They disappeared rapidly, especially the pie!

"I think"—(thought the Duchess to herself)—"I *think* it would be wiser if I helped myself to pie; though Ribby did not seem to notice anything when she was cutting it. What very small fine pieces it has cooked into! I did not remember that I had minced it up so fine; I suppose this is a quicker oven than my own."

"How fast Duchess is eating!" thought Ribby to herself, as she buttered her fifth muffin.

The pie-dish was emptying rapidly! Duchess had had four helps already, and was fumbling with the spoon.

"A little more bacon, my dear Duchess?" said Ribby.

"Thank you, my dear Ribby; I was only feeling for the patty-pan."

WHERE IS THE PATTY-PAN?

"The patty-pan? my dear Duchess?"

"The patty-pan that held up the pie-crust," said Duchess, blushing under her black coat.

"Oh, I didn't put one in, my dear Duchess," said Ribby; "I don't think that it is necessary in pies made of mouse."

Duchess fumbled with the spoon — "I can't find it!" she said anxiously.

"There isn't a patty-pan," said Ribby, looking perplexed.

"Yes, indeed, my dear Ribby; where can it have gone to?" said Duchess.

"There most certainly is not one, my dear Duchess. I disapprove of tin articles in puddings and pies. It is most undesirable — (especially when people swallow in lumps!)" she added in a lower voice.

Duchess looked very much alarmed, and continued to scoop the inside of the pie-dish.

"My Great-aunt Squintina (grand-mother of Cousin Tabitha Twitchit) — died of a thimble in a Christmas plum-pudding. *I* never put any article of metal in *my* puddings or pies."

Duchess looked aghast, and tilted up the pie-dish.

"I have only four patty-pans, and they are all in the cup-board."

Duchess set up a howl.

"I shall die! I shall die! I have swallowed a patty-pan! Oh, my dear Ribby, I do feel so ill!"

"It is impossible, my dear Duchess; there was not a patty-pan."

Duchess moaned and whined and rocked herself about.

"Oh I feel so dreadful, I have swallowed a patty-pan!"

"There was *nothing* in the pie," said Ribby severely.

"Yes there *was*, my dear Ribby, I am sure I have swallowed it!"

"Let me prop you up with a pillow, my dear Duchess; where do you think you feel it?"

"Oh I do feel so ill *all over* me, my dear Ribby; I have swallowed

a large tin patty-pan with a sharp
scalloped edge!"

"Shall I run for the doctor? I will
just lock up the spoons!"

"Oh yes, yes! fetch Dr. Maggotty,
my dear Ribby; he is a Pie himself,

he will certainly understand."

Ribby settled Duchess in an arm-chair before the fire, and went out and hurried to the village to look for the doctor.

She found him at the smithy.

He was occupied in putting rusty nails into a bottle of ink, which he had obtained at the post office.

"Gammon? ha! HA!" said he, with his head on one side.

Ribby explained that her guest had swallowed a patty-pan.

"Spinach? ha! HA!" said he, and accompanied her with alacrity.

He hopped so fast that Ribby had

DR. MAGGOTTY'S MIXTURE

to run. It was most conspicuous. All the village could see that Ribby was fetching the doctor.

"I *knew* they would over-eat themselves!" said Cousin Tabitha Twitchit.

But while Ribby had been hunting for the doctor — a curious thing had happened to Duchess, who had been left by herself, sitting before the fire, sighing and groaning and feeling very unhappy.

"How *could* I have swallowed it! such a large thing as a patty-pan!"

She got up and went to the table, and felt inside the pie-dish again with a spoon.

"No; there is no patty-pan, and I put one in; and nobody has eaten pie except me, so I must have swallowed it!"

She sat down again, and stared mournfully at the grate. The fire crackled and danced, and something sizz-z-zled!

Duchess started! She opened the door of the *top* oven; out came a rich steamy flavour of veal and ham, and there stood a fine brown pie — and through a hole in the top of the pie-crust there was a glimpse of a little tin patty-pan!

Duchess drew a long breath —

"Then I must have been eating Mouse!... No wonder I feel ill ... But perhaps I should feel worse if I had really swallowed a patty-pan!" Duchess reflected — "What a very awkward thing to have to explain to Ribby! I think I will put *my* pie in the back-yard and say nothing about it. When I go home, I will run round and take it away." She put it outside the back door, and sat down again by the fire, and shut her eyes; when Ribby arrived with the doctor, she seemed fast asleep.

"Gammon, ha, Ha?" said the doctor.

"I am feeling very much better," said Duchess, waking up with a jump.

"I am truly glad to hear it! He has brought you a pill, my dear Duchess!"

"I think I should feel *quite* well if he only felt my pulse," said Duchess, backing away from the magpie, who sidled up with something in his beak.

"It is only a bread-pill, you had much better take it; drink a little milk, my dear Duchess!"

"Gammon? Gammon?" said the doctor, while Duchess coughed and choked.

"Don't say that again!" said Ribby, losing her temper—"Here, take this bread and jam, and get out into the yard!"

"Gammon and Spinach! ha ha HA!" shouted Dr. Maggotty triumphantly outside the back door . . .

"I am feeling very much better, my dear Ribby," said Duchess. "Do you not think that I had better go home before it gets dark?"

"Perhaps it might be wise, my

dear Duchess. I will lend you a nice warm shawl, and you shall take my arm."

"I would not trouble you for worlds; I feel wonderfully better. One pill of Dr. Maggotty—"

"Indeed it is most admirable, if it has cured you of a patty-pan! I will call directly after breakfast to ask how you have slept."

Ribby and Duchess said good-bye affectionately, and Duchess started home. Half-way up the lane she stopped and looked back; Ribby had gone in and shut her door. Duchess slipped through the fence, and ran round to the back of Ribby's house and peeped into the yard.

Upon the roof of the pig-stye sat Dr. Maggotty and three jackdaws. The jackdaws were eating pie-crust, and the magpie was drinking gravy out of a patty-pan.

"Gammon, ha, HA!" he shouted when he saw Duchess's little black nose peeping round the corner.

Duchess ran home feeling uncommonly silly!

When Ribby came out for a pailful of water to wash up the tea-things, she found a pink and white pie-dish lying smashed in the middle of the yard. The patty-pan

SO THERE REALLY *WAS* A PATTY-PAN

was under the pump, where Dr. Maggotty had considerately left it.

Ribby stared with amazement — "Did you ever see the like! so there really *was* a patty-pan? . . . But *my* patty-pans are all in the kitchen cupboard. Well I never did! . . . Next time I want to give a party — I will invite Cousin Tabitha Twitchit!"

THE END

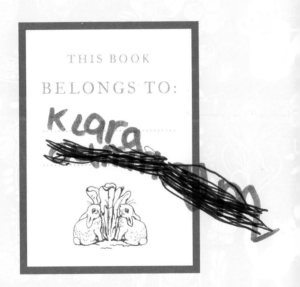

THIS BOOK

BELONGS TO:

Klara

THE TALE OF
The Flopsy Bunnies

THE TALE OF
THE FLOPSY BUNNIES

BY

BEATRIX POTTER

A PETER RABBIT™
110th Anniversary Edition

FREDERICK WARNE

FOR ALL LITTLE FRIENDS OF
MR. McGREGOR & PETER & BENJAMIN

FREDERICK WARNE

Published by the Penguin Group
Penguin Books Ltd., 80 Strand, London WC2R 0RL, England
Penguin Group (USA) Inc., 375 Hudson Street, New York, New York 10014, USA
Penguin Group (Australia), 250 Camberwell Road, Camberwell,
Victoria 3124, Australia (a division of Pearson Australia Group Pty. Ltd.)
Penguin Group (Canada), 90 Eglinton Avenue East, Suite 700, Toronto,
Ontario M4P 2Y3, Canada (a division of Pearson Penguin Canada Inc.)
Penguin Books India Pvt. Ltd., 11 Community Centre, Panchsheel Park, New Delhi—110 017, India
Penguin Group (NZ), 67 Apollo Drive, Rosedale, Auckland 0632,
New Zealand (a division of Pearson New Zealand Ltd.)
Penguin Books (South Africa) (Pty.) Ltd, 24 Sturdee Avenue, Rosebank, Johannesburg 2196, South Africa

Penguin Books Ltd., Registered Offices: 80 Strand, London WC2R 0RL, England

Website: www.peterrabbit.com

First published by Frederick Warne in 1909
First published with reset text and new reproductions
of Beatrix Potter's illustrations in 2002
This edition published in 2011

003 - 10 9 8 7 6 5 4 3

Colour reproduction by
EAE Creative Colour Ltd, Norwich
Printed and bound in China

PUBLISHER'S NOTE

The Tale of The Flopsy Bunnies has remained much the same since the first edition was published in 1909. Beatrix Potter made one change to artwork for later editions after proposals to translate the books into French. In one of the original illustrations there was a sign advertising the business of 'Peter Rabbit and Mother, Florists'. To avoid problems with translation, Beatrix created a new illustration and replaced the sign with Peter himself hard at work in the garden. The revised image can be seen in this edition on page 10.

IT IS SAID that the effect of eating too much lettuce is "soporific".

I have never felt sleepy after eating lettuces; but then *I* am not a rabbit.

They certainly had a very soporific effect upon the Flopsy Bunnies!

WHEN Benjamin Bunny grew up, he married his Cousin Flopsy. They had a large family, and they were very improvident and cheerful.

I do not remember the separate names of their children; they were generally called the "Flopsy Bunnies".

As there was not always quite enough to eat — Benjamin used to borrow cabbages from Flopsy's brother, Peter Rabbit, who kept a nursery garden.

SOMETIMES Peter Rabbit had no cabbages to spare.

WHEN this happened, the
Flopsy Bunnies went across the
field to a rubbish heap, in the
ditch outside Mr. McGregor's
garden.

MR. McGREGOR's rubbish heap was a mixture. There were jam pots and paper bags, and mountains of chopped grass from the mowing machine (which always tasted oily), and some rotten vegetable marrows and an old boot or two. One day —oh joy!—there were a quantity of overgrown lettuces, which had "shot" into flower.

THE FLOPSY BUNNIES simply stuffed lettuces. By degrees, one after another, they were overcome with slumber, and lay down in the mown grass.

Benjamin was not so much overcome as his children. Before going to sleep he was sufficiently wide awake to put a paper bag over his head to keep off the flies.

THE little Flopsy Bunnies slept delightfully in the warm sun. From the lawn beyond the garden came the distant clacketty sound of the mowing machine. The blue-bottles buzzed about the wall, and a little old mouse picked over the rubbish among the jam pots.

(I can tell you her name, she was called Thomasina Tittlemouse, a wood-mouse with a long tail.)

SHE rustled across the paper bag, and awakened Benjamin Bunny.

The mouse apologized profusely, and said that she knew Peter Rabbit.

WHILE she and Benjamin were talking, close under the wall, they heard a heavy tread above their heads; and suddenly Mr. McGregor emptied out a sackful of lawn mowings right upon the top of the sleeping Flopsy Bunnies! Benjamin shrank down under his paper bag. The mouse hid in a jam pot.

THE little rabbits smiled sweetly in their sleep under the shower of grass; they did not awake because the lettuces had been so soporific.

They dreamt that their mother Flopsy was tucking them up in a hay bed.

Mr. McGregor looked down after emptying his sack. He saw some funny little brown tips of ears sticking up through the lawn mowings. He stared at them for some time.

PRESENTLY a fly settled on one of them and it moved.

Mr. McGregor climbed down on to the rubbish heap—

"One, two, three, four! five! six leetle rabbits!" said he as he dropped them into his sack. The Flopsy Bunnies dreamt that their mother was turning them over in bed. They stirred a little in their sleep, but still they did not wake up.

MR. MCGREGOR tied up the sack and left it on the wall.

He went to put away the mowing machine.

WHILE he was gone, Mrs. Flopsy Bunny (who had remained at home) came across the field.

She looked suspiciously at the sack and wondered where everybody was?

THEN the mouse came out of her jam pot, and Benjamin took the paper bag off his head, and they told the doleful tale.

Benjamin and Flopsy were in despair, they could not undo the string.

But Mrs. Tittlemouse was a resourceful person. She nibbled a hole in the bottom corner of the sack.

THE little rabbits were pulled out
and pinched to wake them.

Their parents stuffed the empty
sack with three rotten vegetable
marrows, an old blacking-brush
and two decayed turnips.

THEN they all hid under a bush and watched for Mr. McGregor.

Mr. McGregor came back and picked up the sack, and carried it off.

He carried it hanging down, as if it were rather heavy.

The Flopsy Bunnies followed at a safe distance.

THEY watched him go into his house.

And then they crept up to the window to listen.

MR. McGREGOR threw down the sack on the stone floor in a way that would have been extremely painful to the Flopsy Bunnies, if they had happened to have been inside it.

They could hear him drag his chair on the flags, and chuckle—

"One, two, three, four, five, six leetle rabbits!" said Mr. McGregor.

"Eh? What's that? What have they been spoiling now?" enquired Mrs. McGregor.

"One, two, three, four, five, six leetle fat rabbits!" repeated Mr. McGregor, counting on his fingers — "one, two, three —"

"Don't you be silly; what do you mean, you silly old man?"

"In the sack! one, two, three, four, five, six!" replied Mr. McGregor.

(The youngest Flopsy Bunny got upon the window-sill.)

MRS. McGREGOR took hold of the sack and felt it. She said she could feel six, but they must be *old* rabbits, because they were so hard and all different shapes.

"Not fit to eat; but the skins will do fine to line my old cloak."

"Line your old cloak?" shouted Mr. McGregor — "I shall sell them and buy myself baccy!"

"Rabbit tobacco! I shall skin them and cut off their heads."

MRS. MCGREGOR untied the
sack and put her hand inside.

When she felt the vegetables
she became very very angry.
She said that Mr. McGregor
had "done it a purpose".

AND Mr. McGregor was very angry too. One of the rotten marrows came flying through the kitchen window, and hit the youngest Flopsy Bunny.

It was rather hurt.

THEN Benjamin and Flopsy thought that it was time to go home.

So Mr. McGregor did not get his tobacco, and Mrs. McGregor did not get her rabbit skins.

But next Christmas Thomasina Tittlemouse got a present of enough rabbit-wool to make herself a cloak and a hood, and a handsome muff and a pair of warm mittens.

THE END